Produced by
Allegra Publishing Ltd London
for Caxton Publishing Group

Editor : Felicia Law
Designer : Karen Radford

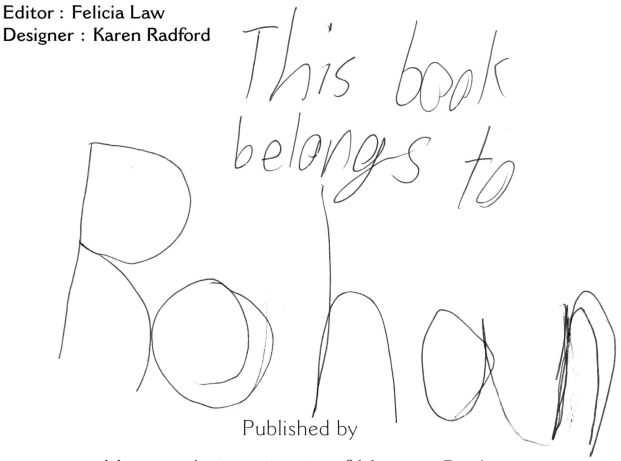
This book belongs to Rohan

Published by

Mercury Junior an imprint of Mercury Books

20 Bloomsbury Street

London WC1B 3JH, UK

ISBN 9781845600440

The Three Pirates
The Griffin

Sheila McCullagh

Illustrated by Rupert van Wyk

Mercury Junior
20 Bloomsbury St, London, WC1B 3JH , UK

Once upon a time, there were three pirates. Their names were Roderick, Greg and Ben. Roderick was fat and short and he huffed and puffed a lot. Greg was tall and thin and a bit forgetful. And Ben was a dreamer, but he had to keep his eyes firmly on the other two!

Roderick the Red pirate

Greg the Green pirate

6

The three pirates each had a sack full of gold, a pair of fine boots and a hat, and they each had a fine sailing ship. The pirates decided to sail away and find an island where they could hide their gold, but quite by accident they all chose the same island. And that's when the trouble began! (Roderick stole Greg's gold, but he's not going to tell him, of course!) The pirates were out in a storm, and their ships were wrecked.

You can read about this adventure in **Pirate Gold**.

But now they are about to meet up again and things are about to get even worse...

Ben the Blue pirate

The island where the pirates were shipwrecked
was very big. There were trees there, and there was
water. There were rocks in the sea where the ships of
Greg and Roderick had been broken in the storm;
and far out to sea, there was a very big rock. It was
so big that it seemed more like a small island.

Ben went to have a look at his ship where it lay on the sand. He looked at it and sighed.

"It's going to be hard to get her into the water again," he said. He didn't feel at all happy. "I don't want to stay on this island with the red pirate and the green pirate, I just don't know what to do. Perhaps they'll want to go to other islands, and I can take them there in my ship. But I know one thing, I can't go to Acrooacree with Roderick and Greg. I don't want to take them there, and they wouldn't want to go." And he sighed again.

He stood there for a long
time, just looking at the ship.
Then he went off to look at the island.

The sun shone in the sky, but Ben couldn't feel happy.
He walked by the water and under the trees, and then
came back to the sand again. He looked across the sand
to the sea. There was a large stone not far away, down by
the sea. The sea tossed round the stone on one side,
and the waves tossed white on the blue water. It was just
a stone, a long black slab. But there was something
on top of it – something which shone in the sunshine.
The something was a deep yellow-gold shining in the sun.

10

Ben went softly across the sand up to the stone, and
looked. There on the stone a creature lay asleep.
He looked very fine, for he was a deep golden-yellow.
He lay very still. He lay there fast asleep in the sunshine.
He had a long tail, and at first, Ben thought he looked
something like a big lion. He was as big as Ben.
Indeed he was bigger.

Then Ben saw that he had two big golden-yellow wings, which were over his sides. Ben could not see his face at all, because it was hidden under his wings as he lay there asleep. Ben stood very still. And then the creature lifted his head. He lifted his wings, and lifted his head from under his wings, and looked up. His eyes were golden, and he had pointed ears, and his mouth turned up at the corners. The creature looked up and saw Ben.

Ben didn't feel at all frightened. The creature didn't look as if he wanted to frighten anyone. He just sat there, very still.

And then he smiled. He smiled a very wide smile, and the corners of his mouth turned right up.

"Hello, pirate," said the creature.

"Hello, creature," said Ben, and waved his fist.
(Pirates always wave their fists when they meet anyone.)

Ben smiled a little too. He couldn't help it. The creature
looked such a very fine golden-yellow, there on the stone
in the sunshine. The creature smiled a wide smile.
Ben began to feel happy.

"Creature," he said, "creature, what are you?
I've never seen a creature like you before."

"You're right, pirate," said the creature. "You've never
seen a creature like me before. For I am the Griffin."
And this time he smiled such a very wide
smile that the corners of his mouth
turned up and nearly touched his
pointed ears!

"I'm not just a Griffin," said the Griffin. "I'm THE Griffin –
the Griffin-of-the-Rock. And I'm not like any other
creature."

"The rock?" asked Benjamin. "The rock out there,
far away in the sea?"

"That's right," said the Griffin. "That's my rock.
This stone," (and he touched the stone where he was
sitting with his claw), "this is just a stone. But the rock
out there in the sea is my rock. I call it the Rock.
And I am the Griffin-of-the-Rock."

15

The blue pirate smiled. It was the first time since the storm that he had felt happy. He couldn't help it. There was something about the Griffin which made Ben feel better whenever he looked at him. Perhaps it was his golden-yellow wings, which shone in the sunshine. Perhaps it was his golden eyes or his wide smile.

"I'm glad I met you, Griffin," said Ben. "Before I met you, I wasn't feeling very happy."

"No?" asked the Griffin. "Was it the storm? I think I saw your ship on her side in the sand. Perhaps I could help. Is the ship broken?"

"Well, it's not just the ship. It's the pirates," said Ben. "The red pirate and the green pirate are on the island too. Their ships went down in the storm and were broken on the rocks. I don't know what to do now. I was going to find Acrooacree. But what am I to do about Roderick and Greg? I can't take them to Acrooacree, and they wouldn't want to go there. But they can't be left here."
Ben looked at the Griffin.

"Don't worry," said the Griffin. He smiled again, and this time Ben felt as if big black clouds where lifting from him. "It'll be all right. The first thing to do is to get your ship back on the sea, and after that, we'll think about it. I have to go back to the Rock now, but I will come again."

And with that the Griffin stood up, and shook his wings.
"The sun is setting, pirate," he said. "And I'm going now.
I'll be back here again in the morning. When the sun
comes up in the morning, I shall come back to this
island." And he shook his wings again, and was gone
like a flash of gold in the sky.

18

Ben stood and looked out to sea till he saw, far away,
a flash of gold on the big rock. The sun set and the red
sky shone on the red sea. The sun went down. It was
as if the sun went down right under the sea. But even
when the sun had gone, it seemed to Ben that, far away
out to sea, he could still see a flash of gold.

19

Roderick the Red had had a good night. Before it grew dark, he had gone over to Ben's ship as it lay there on its side on the sand. And he was still asleep in the ship when Ben came back across the island to look for him.

Ben looked in his ship and saw Roderick the Red asleep there. Roderick was sleeping very deeply, and puffing and blowing.

"Hello!" shouted Ben in Roderick's ear.

Roderick moved, rolled over, and went to sleep again.

"Hello!" said Ben, still louder.

20

Roderick puffed hard, but he didn't move again,

and he didn't wake up.

"HELLO!" said Ben, very loudly indeed. "WAKE UP!"

Roderick woke up.

"Oh," he said. "It's you, is it?" He sighed deeply.

"Yes," said Ben. "Good morning. It's time to wake up."

He waved his fist in the air. (Pirates always wave their

fists when they meet.)

Roderick lifted his hand, waved his fist about his head,

and sighed again. "Give me your hand, and pull me up."

Ben gave him his hand, and pulled very hard, and

Roderick pulled himself up.

"Good," said Roderick. "That's fine. Now then!"
He shook himself. "Is it a fine morning?"

"A very fine morning," said Ben. "The sun is just up
over the sea, and the wind is blowing softly,
and the waves are white on the sand."

"Well," said Roderick. "Let's have something to eat,
and then we'll see what we can do with this ship."

"There's something to eat in the ship," said Ben,
"and there are coconuts under the trees, too. I'll get
something for each of us, and we'll have it here.
Where's Greg?"

"I don't know," said Roderick. "Still talking, I think.
I left him in the dark, still talking.
Don't worry about Greg."

"I'll go and find him first," said Ben.
"Then I'll come with you,"
said Roderick.

So the pirates set out across the sand, and not very far
away they found Greg.

23

Greg the Green had not had such a good night. He had
fallen asleep all right, but each time he fell asleep,
something happened, and he woke up; and then he had
to go to sleep all over again. The first time he fell asleep,
he went to sleep with his head on a stone, and then he
moved in his sleep, and his head fell off the stone, and
he woke up. So then he went to sleep under a tree; but it
was a coconut tree, and just as he got to sleep, a coconut
fell on him, and he woke up again. Then he went to sleep
under a rock, but this time he was too near the sea, and
in the night the sea came in, and a wave broke over him,
and he woke up. Then he went to sleep on the sand, as
Ben had done, and this time nothing happened, and he
slept till morning.

24

The sun woke him up, and he'd just had time to shake himself, when he saw Ben and Roderick coming across the sand. Each pirate waved his fist (as pirates do when they meet) and Ben and Roderick came up to Greg.

"Hello," said Ben.

"Good morning," said Roderick.

"Hello," said Greg. "But it's not a good morning."

"No?" asked Ben.

"No," said Greg.

Roderick sighed. "That's just like Greg," he said.

"Did you sleep?" asked Ben.

"Not very well," said Greg. "You see, when darkness came, I found a big stone. At first I went to sleep with my head on the stone; but it fell off ... "

"It's still on as far as I can see," said Roderick.

"But do stop talking. It's time for breakfast."

25

All three pirates went back to the ship to have something to eat. On the way they picked up some coconuts. The sun was up by this time, shining down on the island as they all sat there by the ship on the sand. And all the time, as they were sitting there, Ben was looking out to sea and thinking about the Griffin. He didn't say anything about the Griffin to the other two pirates. He didn't know what they would think, and he wanted the Griffin to be there himself before anyone said much about him.

It wasn't very long before Ben saw a flash of gold, like lightning in the blue sky, and there was the Griffin, standing before them on the sands. His golden-yellow wings shone as they had done the day before. He held them by his golden-yellow sides, and sat back on the sand.

"Hello, pirates," he said.

The Griffin smiled at Ben, and again it seemed that the sun was shining inside the Griffin. His wings seemed to flash in the sunshine. Ben smiled too. He got up, and waved his fist. "Hello, Griffin," he said.

The other two pirates stood up as well, but they were too surprised to say anything.

27

"This is Roderick the Red," said Ben. "And this is Greg the Green."

He pointed first at Roderick, and then at Greg as he said their names. (Pirates do point at people when they say their names. But pirates are allowed to point.) Roderick and Greg waved their fists in the air (Pirates always wave their fists when they meet anyone, whether he's another pirate or not.)

"Hello, creature," said Roderick.

"Hello, creature," said Greg. "What are you?"

"I am the Griffin," said the Griffin.
"The Griffin-of-the-Rock."

"What are you doing here?" asked Roderick.

"This is my island," said the Griffin. "And far away out to sea you can see my rock."

"I've never seen a griffin before," said Greg.

"This is THE Griffin," said Ben. "The Griffin-of-the Rock."

"I've never seen a griffin on a rock, and I've never seen a griffin off a rock," said Greg.

"THE Griffin-of-the-Rock," said Ben.

"That's what I said – a griffin," said Greg.

The Griffin smiled at Ben. "I can see that you're right about Roderick and Greg", he said.

"Right about what?" asked Roderick.

"You want to get away from this island, don't you?" asked the Griffin.

"We do indeed," said Roderick. "We don't like this island."

"Then let's take a look at Ben's ship first," said the Griffin. "Let's see what we can do about it."

They all went over the sand to the ship.
She lay there on her side.

"It'll take days to mend the holes in the sails,"
said Greg. "It'll take days to get her into the water
again. Days and days. Even years. And perhaps there's
a hole in her side too."

"There is no hole in her side," said Ben. "She didn't
touch the rocks. She was just tossed up here on
the sand."

"Perhaps she'll never sail again," said Greg.

"I think she will," said the Griffin. And he looked
over the ship. "Now then," he said. "Cut down some of
the trees, and lay them on the sand in front of the ship.
Make a slipway of trees for the ship, and we will roll
her over the trees, and down to the water."

Ben smiled. "You're clever, Griffin," he said.

31

"Now, we'll cut down the trees. That's the first thing
to be done. Then we must carry the trees down here on
to the sand. And then we can roll the ship over the trees
to the water."

Ben and Greg and the Griffin set to work, and they cut
down a tree and then another. They all worked very hard,
and Roderick stood by, and told them what to do.
They worked very hard, and by the time the sun was
setting, they had cut down all the trees they wanted,
and put them on the sand, so that they'd roll the
ship over them to the water first thing
in the morning.

As the sea grew red in the setting sun,

the Griffin looked up, and smiled at the pirates.

"Good-night, pirates," he said. "I must go now."

"Good-night, Griffin," said Ben. "Shall we see you

in the morning?"

"You'll see me in the morning," said the Griffin.

"Don't worry. I'll be here first thing."

"Good-night, Griffin," said Roderick and Greg.

All three pirates stood and waved their fists as the

Griffin lifted his wings and went back to his rock, like

a flash of golden lightning over the dark sea.

As he had promised, the Griffin came back to the island just as the sun came up. The pirates were still asleep, but the Griffin woke them, and they worked on. Roderick the Red worked too, but he didn't work very hard. Again they worked all day, and pulled the ship over the trees which lay on the sand, and in the end she touched the water.

"Now!" said the Griffin. "One good, hard pull, and she'll be in the sea. Pull!"

The pirates pulled, and the Griffin pulled too. The pirates all puffed and blew, and they all got very hot.

"Pull harder!" said the Griffin.

They pulled and pulled, and the ship moved a little more.

And then – splash! splash! SPLASH! The ship was in the water again, no longer on her side, but the right way up.

"Good!" said the Griffin. (The pirates were too hot
and too puffed to say anything.) "Good! Now we'll get
the sails mended, and then you can sail away when
you want to. It'll take some days, but we can do it."

The pirates worked hard for days, mending the sails,
and getting coconuts on the ship to eat, as well as
fresh water.

At last the day came when the ship was ready.

"Now we're ready to sail away!" said Roderick.
"The sails are mended and the ship's all right. We'll all
sail far away and find islands where there is gold. We
must find more gold than any other pirates. We'll sail
away in the morning."

"We'll find jewels as well," said Greg. "We'll find rubies
and sapphires and emeralds. Perhaps we'll find the
jewels I hid on my island …"

The red pirate lifted his fist. Greg really did annoy him.

"If you want to find gold and jewels," said the Griffin, "I can tell you where there's an island where there's more gold and jewels than you've ever seen before."

"Where is this island?" asked Roderick and Greg.

"It's far away, across the sea. But it's a very fine island indeed. A big island. The Mer-people live among the rocks there, and in the sea around the islands. You will see mermaids and mermen there, on the rocks and on the sands. And they have jewels – emeralds and rubies and sapphires – more jewels than you've ever seen, or will ever see again. And they have gold there, more gold than you've ever seen before."

"We'll go there," said Roderick.

"But there's just one thing,"
said the Griffin.

"There's always something," said Greg.

"What is it?" asked Roderick.

"It's this," said the Griffin. "You can go *on* to the island.
The Mer-people will be glad to see pirates, and you'll
like it there. But if you go on to the island, you can
never get *off* it again. If you so much as touch the rocks
and sand, you must stay there always.
You can never sail away again.

But you'll never want to sail away again, Roderick.
You'll like it there. You'll have more gold than you know
what do with. And you'll be happy there, too, Greg.
You'll have more jewels than you've ever seen before."

39

"We'll go and see this island," said Roderick. "And if it's as you say, we'll stay there. If we found such an island, we'd never want to sail away again."

"Very well," said the Griffin. "Since Ben will be taking you in his ship, I'll tell him which way to go. Good-night, pirates."

"Good-night, Griffin," said Roderick. "We'll go to this island and have more gold and jewels than any other pirates."

"And the Mer-people will help us?" asked Greg.

"Yes, the Mer-people will help you. Don't worry, Greg," said the Griffin. "Good-night."

The Griffin led Ben away.

"Don't worry, Ben. Things aren't as bad as
you think. You'll go alone to find Acrooacree,
and I have three things here to give you.
Here's the first thing."

The Griffin put one hand under his wing and pulled out
a little shining mirror. It shone silver and gold.

"This is a mirror, Ben," said the Griffin." If ever you don't
know which way to go, look in the mirror and you'll see
the way you've come. And when you see the way back,
then you'll know the way forward."

"Thank you, Griffin," said Ben. "I'll do as you say."
Ben carefully put the mirror away.

"And take this candle, Ben," said the Griffin.
"It will shine whenever you want a light to see
your way. This is a candle that never goes out."

"Thank you, Griffin," said Ben. He took the candle and put it away.

"And here's another thing," said the Griffin. He lifted his left wing, and from under his wing he pulled out a little golden flute.

"Listen!" he said, "and I'll play to you." He blew into the flute, and played a tune. "Listen, Ben!" And he played the tune again. The tune seemed to come from very far away, across the sea.

The Griffin gave Ben the flute. "You play it," he said. Ben took the flute and played the tune.

"That's right," said the Griffin. "Now, take this flute with you, and if you ever want me, play this tune on the flute. I'll hear it wherever you are. Whether you are hidden among the islands, far away across the sea, or even on Acrooacree, when I hear the flute, I will come.

And there's just one more thing, Ben.
If you want to sail away and not run the ship on the rocks, you must listen to the Mer-people singing. You couldn't hear them before. But now I'll blow softly in your ears and then you'll hear them. When you hear the Mer-people singing loudly, you'll know that you are near rocks, and then you must turn the ship away."

The Griffin put his hands on Ben's head, and blew softly into his ears, first into Ben's right ear, and then into his left.

43

"And now, good-night, Ben," the Griffin said. "The moon
is up and I must go back to my rock. But I'll be here
again in the morning. You have the mirror and the candle
and the flute, and now you can hear the Mer-people
singing. All will be well, and you'll find Acrooacree."

And with that the Griffin lifted his wings
and smiled his wide smile, and was gone.

Ben stood looking out over the sea for a long time.
The sea lay silver before him. At first the night seemed
still, but as he stood, he could hear singing.
It came from far away, far away across the rocks,
where the water splashed silver in the moonlight.

"It's the Mer-people singing," said Ben,
and as he listened, he could hear their song.

"Roo-a-ree, roo-a-ree,
Over the waves and under the sea,
Over and under the waves go we.
Roo-a-run, roo-a-run,
Golden waves in the light of the sun,
Till the light fades and the day is done.
Roo-a-roon, roo-a-roon,
Silver waves in the light of the moon,
Darkness fades and the day comes soon.
Roo-a-ree, roo-a-ree,
Over the waves and the under the sea,
Over and under the waves go we."

And as Ben listened, sleep came over him, and he lay
down on the sand, just as he had done on his first night
on the island. He went to sleep with the singing of
the Mer-people still in his ears.